DRAGON CHILD

The
Emerald Quest

To Mary and Fran, true DragonFriends

First published 2012 by A & C Black,
an imprint of Bloomsbury Publishing Plc
50 Bedford Square
London WC1B 3DP

www.bloomsbury.com

ISBN 978-1-4081-7412-8

A CIP catalogue for this book is available from the British Library.

Printed and Bound by CPI Group (UK) Ltd, Croydon CR0 4YY

1 3 5 7 9 10 8 6 4 2

MIX
Paper from
responsible sources
FSC® C020471

DRAGON CHILD

The Emerald Quest

GILL VICKERY

A & C BLACK
AN IMPRINT OF BLOOMSBURY
LONDON NEW DELHI NEW YORK SYDNEY

Northern Sea

Fellhof

East Eldkeiler mts.

Drakelow mts

Eastern Sea

Kulafoss

Drangur

Holmurholt

Askarlend

Roornhof

Southern Sea

Prologue

The little village of Hamar had never heard such a tumult! A great roaring echoed round the houses and a hot wind shrieked through the narrow streets. People hurried to see what was happening.

'Stay inside the house,' Tia's father ordered as he ran to join the other villagers.

Tia scrambled onto a chair so that she could look out of the window. In the fields on the edge of the village was a huge red dragon, bellowing and spouting flames.

Tia had seen lots of dragons, but she'd never seen one lose its temper before. Why was he in Hamar? And why was he so angry?

She wanted to find out. She scurried out of the house and ran to the corn field. There, she hid behind a hedge and watched as the red dragon turned round and round, churning up the corn.

'Where is Ondine?' he roared at the villagers.

Tia's father stepped forward and bowed.

'I am Elio, mighty one,' he said. 'Ondine is my wife. What do you want with her?'

The dragon hissed, hot little flames licking his cruel mouth. 'She is one of the scheming thieves who have stolen our jewels of power!'

The villagers gasped in horror.

'No! Ondine would never steal from the DragonQueen!' Elio said.

'Then why isn't she here?' roared the dragon.

'She went to the DragonQueen's Keep to bring a gift – a swan's down coverlet for her new eggs.'

'And there she stole the jewels of power! Where is she now?' the dragon demanded.

'I don't know!' said Elio desperately.

'You lie!' The dragon thundered towards Tia's father, the ground shaking with his angry steps, and snatched up Elio in his claws.

'Stop it!' Tia burst from her hiding place and ran towards the dragon.

'No, Tia! Run!' Elio cried.

Tia took no notice. She beat at the huge scaly foot holding her father.

'Leave my Papa alone!'

The dragon roared again, dropped Tia's father,

and grasped her. She screamed and kicked at the iron-hard claws.

'Enough!' the dragon growled. He turned to Elio. 'Ondine helped take our jewels of power, so I will take your witch-brat.' He gathered himself into a crouch and sprang up and away into the sky.

Far below, Tia saw her father cupping his hands to his mouth.

'I'll find you, Tia!' he called. 'I'll find you and bring you back. Remember!'

His voice faded and the village of Hamar grew smaller as the dragon flew up and up, his huge wings beating with a steady rhythm that boomed in the air.

All of sudden and from out of nowhere, a great blast like an invisible storm sent the dragon spinning over and over in the sky. He flapped his wings frantically in an effort to stay in the air – and he lost his grip on Tia. Down and down she fell, the wind rushing past her, whirling her closer and closer to the ground.

Through her screams, she heard the dragon roar. He was hurtling down towards her, but he was flying again, not falling.

Just as she was about to hit the earth, the dragon scooped her up.

'It was a spell!' the dragon thundered. 'The High Witches have used magic to drive us away from our lands.' He was angrier than ever. He tightened his grip on Tia, wheeled around in the sky and flew swiftly towards the distant Drakelow Mountains.

It was dusk by the time the red dragon landed at the ancient Keep where the dragons had gathered for safety.

'I could not find Ondine, but I have her child,' he said and opened his foot. Tia stumbled out; even though she was tired and afraid of the huge creatures towering over her, she kicked the dragon as hard as she could.

He prodded her forward. 'Bow to the DragonQueen,' he ordered.

Tia bowed solemnly to the golden-green dragon.

'You're very small,' the DragonQueen said. 'How old are you?'

'Old enough not to be scared of dragons!' Tia said. But she began to shiver; it was bitterly cold in the mountains.

'She's shaking – she *is* scared, really,' a young red dragon laughed.

'No I'm not,' Tia said, 'I'm just cold.'

'Be quiet, Torkil,' the DragonQueen said. 'She has spirit; that is surprising in such a young one, though perhaps not in a witch-child.'

'I'm not a witch-child!' Tia insisted.

'Yes you are,' Torkil said. 'Witch-brat!'

'The DragonQueen told you to be quiet.' The mighty red dragon cuffed Torkil. 'Go to your cave.'

The dragons began to speak in strange clicks and hisses that Tia knew was their private language. She wished she knew what they were saying.

The DragonQueen spoke in human language again. 'Freya will take you.'

'I want to go home!' Tia said.

'It isn't possible.' A green dragon grasped the back of Tia's jacket in her mouth and carried her away to a cavern where a copper-coloured dragonet slept in front of a fire.

Freya dropped Tia gently next to him. 'Get warm,' she said, 'while I find something for you to sleep on.'

Tia curled up next to the warm, spicy-smelling hide of the dragonet. Soothed by his even breathing she almost fell asleep herself and didn't protest when Freya picked her up again and placed her on a rocky ledge covered in moss and leaves. Tia burrowed under them so that if she cried Freya wouldn't see her.

Her makeshift bed was prickly but warm. She'd almost fallen asleep when she heard a soft voice say, 'DragonMother? Who is that human child and why is she here?' It was the dragonet.

'Her name is Tia and she's a witch-child,' Freya said.

'Like the High Witches who have the DragonQueen's jewels!' the little dragonet said.

'Yes, Finn, but this child has done nothing wrong. Andgrim couldn't find the High Witches so he stole her away instead.'

'That's kidnapping!'

'Yes,' Freya agreed. 'The DragonQueen wanted Andgrim to take Tia back but the High Witches have cast a powerful spell that prevents dragons from entering the lands of the Six Towns. So the DragonKing and Queen have decided to keep Tia until the spell is broken and the jewels are returned to us.'

'How long will that be?' Finn asked.

Tia held her breath.

'It may be many years,' Freya said. 'Tia will be lonely. Will you be a good DragonBrother to your new foster sister?'

'Yes, I will,' Finn promised.

'Good. Now, go back to sleep.'

Tia heard the scrape of two scaly hides as the dragons settled down together. Very soon all was quiet except for the crackle and hiss of the fire and the soft breathing of the dragons.

Tia watched shadows dance on the cave walls and puzzled over why the dragons thought she was a witch-child. She wasn't, she knew she wasn't – her mother and father were just ordinary villagers. A fierce, empty feeling reminded her that she might not see her parents again for years.

Tears fell down her cheeks. She wiped them away angrily. The dragons would never know she cried, never ever, she promised herself.

At last she fell asleep. In her dreams she heard a voice calling to her – *I'll find you, Tia! I'll find you and bring you back. Remember!* And in her sleep she whispered another promise: 'I won't forget you, Papa. I'll never forget.'

Chapter One

In The Drakelow Mountains

'Ow!' Torkil, the red dragonet, squealed as Tia's pebble bounced off his ear. He wobbled in the air and the dragonet behind flew into him. All the other young dragons had to wheel in the sky to avoid crashing.

'What are you doing, Torkil!' the flying master called, flapping his blue wings angrily. 'Land immediately!'

Torkil landed right in front of the rock Tia was hiding behind. She couldn't resist letting fly with her sling again. This time she hit him on the nose. He roared and spun round.

Tia jumped up from behind the rock, waving her sling. 'Got you!' she yelled.

With another roar, Torkil launched himself at her. She dropped behind the rock and wriggled away down a tunnel as fast as she could. He was too big to squeeze down the narrow passageway.

She wriggled on until she came to a small cavern lit by sunlight streaming from openings in the roof.

The cavern was Tia's secret den. She wound up her sling and put it with her bag of pebbles on a rock shelf. Then she lit her fire, sat on a pile of cushions and picked up her runes book.

She meant to practise writing but she couldn't concentrate.

That morning she'd asked Freya, 'How long have you been my DragonMother?' and Freya had told her, 'Eight years.'

Eight years! She could hardly remember anything from her human past. She did remember her father's voice calling, 'I'll find you, Tia... and bring you back.' But there had been no sign of him.

Perhaps he thinks I died when Andgrim dropped me, she thought sadly.

Tia had forgotten almost everything about her parents – even their names. The only reminder she had was a locket on a chain that she'd been wearing on the day she was kidnapped. Inside were portraits of her mother and father. They looked so kind.

Most of the dragons were good to her. She was respectful to them and never complained about how cold and hard it was living in the mountains. She worked at her lessons and obeyed the dragons' orders.

But she was a hostage: until the witches returned the DragonQueen's necklace with its jewels of power, the dragons wouldn't return Tia to her parents. And Andgrim insisted that she was dangerous. Freya had told her, 'Andgrim's brother, Thor, disappeared trying to recover the necklace from the High Witches. Because some of your family are witches, Andgrim thinks you are dangerous too.'

But Thor had also been Freya's husband, and Freya didn't believe Tia was dangerous. She sighed again and went back to writing runes. The book was almost full; she'd need a new one soon.

She jumped up. The Traders were due to arrive today and Freya would buy her a new book from them. She always made sure the Traders provided everything Tia could want: food and clothes, blankets and cushions, books and pens – even a special iron claw to fit over her finger so that she could write runes in the mud of the teaching cave floor just like the dragonets. The Traders had also taught her how to ride horses, defend herself, light fires, use a sling shot, and cook what she could catch and gather.

She had once asked them to help her escape from Drakelow but they said they couldn't; they needed to be friends with everyone – dragons, ordinary humans and the High Witches – so that they could trade freely in the whole island of Tulay.

Tia ran to Freya's cave, keeping a look out for Torkil on the way. *I hope Torkil and his friends don't take it out on Finn*, she thought. Poor Finn was tormented by the other dragonets because he was her foster brother. Worse than that, he was small for his age and a strange colour. He wasn't green or blue or red as the other dragons were; he was a sort of coppery shade, and he sometimes changed colour, which none of the other dragons did: that really made the dragonets laugh and the more they laughed, the more the colours swirled over Finn's hide.

Tia reached her foster mother's cavern. Although it was huge inside, Freya kept it warm and cosy; a fire burned in a hearth at the centre of the cave and blue smoke curled straight up and out through a vent in the roof. The green dragon was dozing against the far wall when Tia burst in.

Freya opened her glittering golden eyes. 'What's the matter?' she asked kindly. 'Have the dragonets been chasing you again?'

Tia nodded. 'I don't mind,' she said quickly in case Freya thought she was complaining. 'But I don't want Torkil to bother Finn.' She told Freya what she'd done to Torkil.

'That wasn't very sensible,' Freya said getting up from her couch. 'But don't worry about Finn; he'll stand up for himself. And as for you, my little

DragonDaughter...' Freya nudged Tia gently with her nose. 'Be patient.'

Tia climbed up onto the high ledge of her sleeping platform so that she was level with Freya's head, and showed her the runes book.

'You've filled it up,' Freya said.

Tia held up her pen. 'This is wearing out too.'

'Then it's a good thing that the Traders have arrived.'

Tia flung her arms round Freya's green muzzle and kissed her nose. 'Can I go and see them?'

'Of course. I'll go with you as far as the flying ground to see how Finn is doing.'

Tia laughed. Torkil and his friends wouldn't dare torment Finn in front of his mother – Freya was the DragonQueen's sister, after all!

Chapter Two

The Traders Arrive

The Traders had settled on the edge of a grassy plateau encircled by the lower slopes of the Drakelow Mountains. Their tents and stalls, decorated with brightly coloured flags, were pitched close to the dragons' stony caverns in the mountainside. The flags snapped in the spring breeze and the Traders' shaggy little horses happily munched the grass behind the tents.

Tia saw her friends, Kizzy and Florian. She ran up and hugged them.

'My DragonMother's given me some silver coins to buy a new book and a pen.'

The three of them went to Kizzy and Florian's tent where their mother welcomed Tia with a big hug.

'And how is my favourite DragonChild?' she asked with a big smile.

'I'm fine thank you, Zora. I hope you're well too and that trading is good?'

Zora pressed a sweet drink and a piece of honey cake into Tia's hands. 'Trading is not as good as it used to be,' she said sitting down on a bench covered in bright rugs. 'The High Witches have made the country wretched and poor. Now they're quarrelling among themselves and things are getting even worse.'

Zora shook her head angrily. 'Malindra, the High Witch of Drangur, makes things hardest for us. You know that she took the DragonQueen's emerald and uses its power to talk to animals?'

Tia nodded. Drangur was the nearest of the six towns to the Drakelow Mountains, and Malindra's ways were well known.

'She combines it with her magic and forces the animals to do as she wants,' Zora went on. 'She sends dogs and wolves to worry our horses so they take fright easily and then she says they're not worth paying a good price for.'

'We won't sell our horses there now,' Florian blurted out. 'She treats them badly.'

'She sends rats to chew the goods on our stalls,'

Kizzy said. 'They make our leather and cloth look shabby. People think we're trying to cheat them into buying poor goods.'

'Don't you explain to them?' Tia asked.

'They don't want to listen. They're afraid of Malindra's spies,' Zora said.

'Animal spies,' Kizzy added. 'They follow you on quiet little feet. You never know if the dog or cat you see in the street is a pet or one of her spies.'

'The birds are the worst. They can look down on you from anywhere and you never even know it,' Florian said.

'Those High Witches have a lot to answer for,' Zora said. 'But take heart – they are falling out because they can't get the jewels to work properly. They can keep the dragons away from the lands of the six towns, and force the people of Tulay to do what they want, but they have to work hard at it. They don't enjoy their power.' Zora laughed.

'Do you think the High Witches will ever be defeated?' Tia asked.

'Only if the jewels are restored to the DragonQueen,' Zora said. 'Enough of these sad tales. What have you come to the Traders for, Tia?'

'To see my friends,' Tia said, hugging plump Zora. 'And to buy a book for writing in, and a pen.'

'Come with me, we have just the thing!'

Zora's husband, Hanzi, rummaged among the hats and jewellery and jackets and belts and books heaped in piles on his stall. He pulled out a beautiful leaf-green, leather-bound book.

'Oh, it's lovely!' Tia took the book and turned it over and over.

'And here's a pen to go with it,' said Hanzi, holding out a black pen with a pale grey point that shimmered in the sunshine. 'The point is made of silver and will write for as long as you need it to.'

Tia paid him then turned to Zora. 'I'd better go now. Thank you for the honey cake and drink.'

Kizzy caught her hand. 'You'll come to the bonfire tonight to hear the stories and songs, won't you?' she asked.

'Of course, I wouldn't miss it for anything!' Tia said. The Traders were famous for their stories. She waved goodbye and ran home to Freya's cavern.

Chapter Three

Around The Traders' Fire

The bonfire lit the night sky, flames roaring upwards as though they were reaching for the stars.

All two hundred dragons had settled around the plateau; some crouching on the ground and some looking down from their caverns. There were big dragons, nearly five centuries old, and small ones not much older than Tia. Even the Queen and King's little dragonets were allowed to lie between their parents' feet and listen.

The Traders picked up their instruments and Hanzi started to beat a drum, the sound booming round the plateau. The dragons' eyes glittered in the firelight like rubies.

'Listen!' Hanzi said, 'and I'll tell you tales and sing you songs of dragon deeds and dragon lore.'

The dragons roared in pleasure as Hanzi began his stories, and when he sang the old ballads they rumbled along in their deep voices.

At last Hanzi stopped for a drink to soothe his throat. 'Are there any requests?' Zora called out.

'Tell us about Thor's battle with the High Witches and how they stole the Queen's jewels,' a voice called. It was Torkil. He sat opposite Tia and he was looking straight at her with a sly smile on his face.

'Tell us! Tell us!' the other dragonets chanted, flapping their wings and stamping their feet.

So Hanzi told the story of how the six sisters, the High Witches of Holmurholt, took gifts to the DragonQueen in the garden of the Eldkeiler Keep where the Queen guarded her precious eggs.

'The DragonQueen had surrounded her clutch with the necklace bearing the jewels of power,' Hanzi said. 'The sisters stood in a circle round the eggs, one next to each jewel. As they bowed and put their gifts on the ground, each one of them seized a jewel.' Hanzi stooped swiftly and mimed snatching a jewel in both hands.

'They chanted a spell that spirited them away – and the necklace with them!'

The dragons roared. Torkil glared at Tia and she heard him say to the dragonet next to him, 'If she knew what we know!' The other dragonet sniggered.

'She's nothing but a witch-brat!' Torkil clicked.

Tia couldn't say anything; she wasn't supposed to understand the private language of the dragons, but she had learned it by listening carefully.

Hanzi carried on with his story. 'Knowing that the High Witches would use the jewels of power against them, the DragonQueen gathered up her eggs and flew to the safety of this ancient Keep deep in the Drakelow Mountains. The DragonKing and his brothers, Thor and Andgrim, searched all Tulay for the sisters. Thor found them in their home at Holmurholt, but the High Witches raised a wicked spell and Thor was blown far away over the Southern Seas. He has never returned.'

The dragons rumbled and roared again.

'Worse was to come,' Hanzi said. 'The witches used the jewels of power to cast a spell covering the lands of the six towns. It is so terrible and so strong that the dragons can never return until the spell is broken.'

Hanzi raised his arms and began the Chant of Warning that all the dragons knew by heart. One by one they joined in too.

If the jewels of power see a dragon walking warily
On the lost lands of the six towns
The spell will toss them away, tumbling
Like a leaf in a storm.

If the jewels of power see a dragon soaring secretly
Over the lost lands of the six towns
The spell will blast them away, blowing
Like a feather in the wind.

If the jewels of power see a dragon creeping cautiously
Beneath the lost lands of the six towns
The spell will crush them cruelly
Like an eggshell beneath a foot.

By the time Hanzi reached the end all the dragons were chanting loudly: even the littlest dragonet knew the spell-warning by heart. As Tia chanted, she remembered the dreadful force that made Andgrim drop her when he tumbled through the air. She was still very scared of being up high but she was careful not to let any of the dragons know.

'I don't know what she's chanting for,' Torkil clicked to his friend. 'Her mother's one of the High Witches who stole the jewels and cast the spell.'

It couldn't be true!

'Don't be stupid, Torkil.' Finn pushed his way in between the red dragonet and his friend.

'You're the stupid one, freak!' Torkil snarled, and the dragonets laughed as Finn turned bright pink with embarrassment.

'I was there when my DragonFather brought her in,' Torkil hissed. 'I hid behind a rock and I heard it all. Her mother's the youngest of the witch sisters, the one called Ondine.'

Tia couldn't bear to hear any more. She ran to her secret place, her mind whirring with what Torkil had said. Could it be true? Was her own mother one of the High Witches? Tia wouldn't believe it, she wouldn't! But Torkil had sounded so sure.

Tia stayed in her cave for a long time, thinking about Torkil's cruel words. She had to know the truth. She had to ask her DragonMother. Freya would never lie to her.

Freya and Finn were in the cavern, waiting for Tia.

'Where have you been?' Freya asked. 'I was worried when I saw you run away from the storytelling.'

'It was Torkil,' Tia said. 'He said that my mother,

my human mother, is one of the High Witches. Is that true? Did my mother steal the DragonQueen's jewels?'

'How do you know that?' Finn asked.

'I understand your language,' Tia said impatiently. She turned to Freya and demanded, 'Is it true, DragonMother?'

Freya butted Tia gently with her nose. 'Yes, but ...'

Before she could say more Tia choked back a sob and rushed out of the cavern.

Behind her she heard Freya say to Finn, 'Go after her, quickly – make sure she's all right and bring her back.'

Tia ran to her secret cave, slumped against a rock and hugged her knees. She sat for a long time, confused and hurt. More than anything she wanted to go back to her beloved DragonMother and snuggle up to her warm, spicy-smelling hide. But how could she when her human mother had betrayed the dragons? Tia felt sick with shame.

She took out her locket and opened it. How could her mother look so kind when she was a High Witch and a thief?

Tia angrily tried to prise the picture out with her nails but it was too firmly fixed. She couldn't bring herself to scratch it away. After a moment's thought, she tore a scrap out of her rune book and slotted it over the picture. Now she could still see her father but not her treacherous mother. She snapped the locket shut and slipped it under her shirt.

She wrapped a blanket round her shoulders and built a fire. Spring had come to Tulay but the nights were still very cold. Tia didn't care. She'd stay in her secret cave all night. She couldn't go back to Freya and Finn, not yet.

Then she thought, *What if I never go back? What if I run away?* But where could she go?

'I could go to the lands of the six towns,' she said out loud. 'The spell won't affect me, I'm not a dragon.'

And then Tia had another idea. An idea that would prove to Freya – and Torkil and his friends – that Tia was a true DragonChild even though her human mother was a High Witch.

Tia jumped up in excitement and began to push her things into a bag. She would take her clothes, a blanket, her weapons, some food and the money she had left. She would sleep until a few hours before dawn and then creep away while the dragons slept. By the time Freya realised she was gone for good, she would be safely in Drangur, and no dragon would be able to find her.

Chapter Four

The Great Forest of Drangur

Tia crept quietly to where the Traders' horses were tethered. Even in soft leather boots the frozen grass crackled under her feet and made the shaggy little horses look up curiously.

She untied a silver-grey horse.

'Hello, Fari, we're going for a long ride,' she whispered and led him away from the Traders' tents.

Fari tossed his head, his long white mane flopping over his neck, and whickered in excitement. He was the horse Tia had learned to ride on and they were old friends.

Tia bridled Fari and walked him over the grassy

slopes leading away from the mountains. Everywhere looked magical in the white moonlight and Tia's heart beat quickly with excitement. Fari seemed to feel it too and he danced a little, his hooves drumming on the frosty grass.

As soon as she felt far enough away from the Drakelow Keep and the sharp ears of the dragons, Tia jumped on the grey horse's back and squeezed him with her knees. 'Let's gallop, Fari!' she cried, and with a whoop from her and a whinney from Fari, they shot forward, thundering over the frosty grass, towards the Great Forest of Drangur.

Even in the sharp light of morning the forest looked dark and forbidding but Tia didn't let that put her off. She slid from the horse's back and stroked his nose. 'We've got to say goodbye now, Fari,' she said.

Fari blew sweet breath down his nose as if to say, *I understand.*

Tia turned him to face the mountains, knotted the reins and slapped his hindquarters. With a snort he sprang away. Tia watched until he was only a dot on the icy slopes then turned to the Great Forest.

She set off down a twisting path between trees with gnarled old branches draped in shreds of moss. As she went further in, the path grew narrower and more winding, the trees and the undergrowth more dense.

She pulled out her knife and slashed at the brambles that snagged her. Just as she cut herself free from one, a terrible cry like a ghost shrieking rang through the forest. Tia almost dropped her knife in shock.

The cry came again, louder than ever, followed by the sound of laughter.

Tia hurried forward, close to the ground so that she wouldn't be seen, and came to an open space. On the far side were two men. They were prodding sharp sticks at two snow white frost-fox cubs cowering inside a cage.

'Stop it!' Tia cried.

The men looked up in surprise.

'It's a little girl,' one of them sneered with a grin that showed gaps in his yellowed teeth.

'Let those foxes go!' Tia shouted.

The men ignored her.

Angrily, she pulled the sling out of her belt and slipped a pebble into the leather pouch in the middle of the strings. She whirled the sling round her head and then released one of the strings. The pebble flew through the air and hit the first man hard on his hand. He dropped the stick with a yell and spun round.

Tia quickly re-loaded her sling and swung it above her head as the men ran towards her. The strings caught in a branch. Frantically she tugged at it. It wouldn't budge! She let go and started to run but it was too late.

One man caught her jacket and the other her ankles. She wriggled and bit and scratched but the men were strong and had her tied up in no time.

'What'll we do with her?' the first man wondered.

'Take her to Malindra, she'll sort her out,' the other one said.

Malindra – the High Witch of Drangur! Tia knew that once she was in the witch's power it would be impossible to steal the emerald.

'Leave the girl alone!' a voice roared.

The men looked round wildly. For a moment the forest seemed empty and then, out of thin air, Finn appeared right next to them. He stood on his hind legs, crimson with anger, wings stretched as high as they would go, and with flames curling round his sharp teeth.

The men shrieked in terror and ran.

Finn roared and flames hurtled after them,
scorching their hair. They disappeared into the
forest, batting at their smoking hair.

Finn dropped onto all fours and turned back to
his proper coppery colour. He looked very pleased
with himself as he cut Tia free with his claws.

'What are you doing here?' she demanded,
rubbing at her arms and legs.

'DragonMother told me to find you and bring you back,' Finn said. 'I looked for you all night. When you took the horse, I wanted to know what you were up to so I followed you.'

'I'm not going back, not yet anyway,' Tia said stubbornly. 'Not after what Torkil said.'

'He shouldn't have told anyone about... you know... your human mother being a High Witch. It was supposed to be a secret that only the older dragons knew. Torkil got into a lot of trouble.'

'Good. I'm still not going back.'

'All right, but where are you going?' Finn insisted.

'It's a secret,' Tia said and marched off into the trees.

'If you're not going back, I'm coming with you!' Finn said. He followed Tia into the woods, snorting and puffing.

Tia she didn't know whether she was pleased or not that he was following her. It would be good to have her DragonBrother with her, but what would he think when she told him what she was planning to do?

Chapter Five

The Great Spell

By the time Tia and Finn reached the other edge of the forest it was nightfall and they decided to make camp until morning. They built a small fire in front of a low cave. While Tia ate, Finn, who only ate once a week, relaxed by the fire, blowing smoke rings.

'How did you make yourself like the bushes and trees so the trappers couldn't see you?' Tia asked.

'I don't know – it just happened,' Finn said.

'Can you do it on purpose?'

'I'm not sure. I could try.' Finn screwed up his eyes and concentrated. All of a sudden his skin turned to the same colour and pattern as the shadowy rock behind him.

'That's wonderful!' Tia said. 'I can still see you, but the trappers didn't seem to see you at all.'

Tia yawned.

'Don't go to sleep!' Finn said. 'You still haven't told me where you're going – I mean, where *we're* going.'

'I'm going to get the jewels back from the High Witches,' Tia said.

Finn started to laugh. Tia glared at him. He stopped laughing.

'But you're only a girl,' he said, horrified.

'Dragons can't get into the lands of the six towns but humans can – and I'm human.'

'But you're so little! You can't fight the High Witches, they're too powerful.'

'I won't have to fight them because they won't notice me,' Tia said. 'Tomorrow I'm going to Drangur, to get the emerald.'

'You don't even know where it is! How can you steal it?' Finn demanded.

'I can get work in Drangur and find out. Then I can plan how to get it back.'

Smoke rings flew fast from Finn's mouth. He was thinking hard. 'Even if you do manage to steal it, what will you do with it?'

'Nothing. I'm going to steal the jewels, and when I've got them all I'm going to take them back to the

DragonQueen. Then even Torkil will see I'm a real DragonChild and not a witch-brat.'

'What about your mother – your human mother? Are you going to steal the jewel she's got as well?'

'Of course I am!' Tia glared at her DragonBrother. 'I don't care about her – Freya's my real mother, my DragonMother, and I'm her DragonDaughter.'

'But Ondine – '

'I don't want to talk about her any more,' Tia said fiercely.

'All right.' Finn blew a few more smoke rings then said, 'I can't go with you to Drangur or the lands round about it because of the spell.'

'I know,' Tia said. 'But you can help me get there faster than if I was walking.'

'You're not going to ride me!' Finn said in horror, his skin rippling with alarming shades of orange and yellow and green.

'Maybe you can carry me,' Tia teased.

Finn snorted. 'I'll carry your back-pack but you can walk! I'm a dragon, not a horse.'

Tia laughed. 'So you're still going to help me then?'

'I suppose so. DragonMother told me to find you and bring you back. She didn't say it had to be right away.'

41

'That's settled then,' Tia said and yawned again. 'Time to sleep. I need to be wide awake tomorrow.'

They put out the fire, squeezed into the cave and settled down for the night. 'Good night, Finn,' Tia said as she snuggled against him for warmth.

Finn sighed. 'Good night, DragonSister,' he said.

The road to Drangur wound by the edge of the forest. On the other side of the road gentle grassy slopes led to a huge rolling plain. Far away, in the centre of the plain, was a town, surrounded by a thick wall. Rising from the middle of the town was a castle perched on a jagged column of rock.

'That must be Drangur,' Tia said. She had never seen a town or a castle before and she was excited as well as scared. 'I can see people working in the fields.'

The only humans she could remember seeing before were the Traders, and she was curious about other people.

Finn was curious too and peered between the trees to get a better view.

'Stop,' Tia said. 'Someone might see you!'

'No they won't, they're too far away. But if you're worried I'll disguise myself.' In an instant Finn made himself the colour of grass dotted all over with white and yellow and blue wild flowers, and crept out onto the verge at the side of the road.

'Don't go any further!' Tia shrieked. 'You don't know where the spell starts.'

'DragonMother told me that people farm right up to the edges of the spell boundary,' Finn said. 'There's no farmland here.'

It was true – the early green corn and the meadows with sheep and cows were far away in fields edged with low stone walls.

'I bet those walls are the boundary,' Finn said.

At that moment they heard the quick drumming of hooves, and a boy on a brown pony came round a curve in the road. He reined in his pony and stared at Tia in surprise. 'Who are you, Trader?' he said.

Tia realised the boy thought she was a Trader because she was wearing brightly coloured Trader clothes. She decided to use a Trader name.

'I'm Nadya,' she told him, 'and I'm going to Drangur.' She stared as curiously at the boy as he stared at her. He looked strange in his dull grey clothes, and his hair was blond, not red-gold like hers, nor black and curly like most Traders.

'Why are on your own?' he asked.

'I got parted from my parents in a fog when we were coming back from the Drakelow Mountains. They were going to trade in Drangur so I'm going there too, to find them.'

Tia was amazed to find herself inventing such a story. She'd had no idea she could do it. 'If my

parents aren't there I'm going to look for work until they arrive.'

'You were in the Drakelow Mountains?' the boy said, his eyes wide and bright. 'Did you see any dragons?'

Finn sniggered and the pony jumped nervously.

'What was that noise?' the boy said looking straight at where Finn lay on the grass.

Tia was amazed he couldn't see Finn. She could easily see the shape of her DragonBrother, even though his colour matched the ground, but it seemed as though he was completely invisible to the boy.

'I didn't hear anything,' Tia lied. 'I've seen lots of dragons – we trade with them all the time. Haven't you ever seen one?'

The boy shook his head. 'No, because of the great spell the High Witches cast to keep them away. I'd like to see a dragon someday.'

'They're not as special as you'd think,' Tia said. 'The young ones can be very stupid. Tell me, the great spell, where does it start?'

'Where the forest ends. As soon as you step out of the forest and on to the grass, the spell boundary begins.'

'Thank you,' Tia said and the boy trotted away.

Tia hurried to Finn. 'Don't change colour!' she said. 'Just come with me quickly.'

Back at the cave they talked about what the boy had said.

'He must be wrong,' Finn said. 'The spell says, "If the jewels of power see a dragon walking warily on the lost lands of the six towns – the spell will toss them away, tumbling like a leaf in a storm." I walked on the grass verge and nothing happened.'

Tia frowned and silently marched up and down in front of the cave, thinking.

'That's it!' she said at last. Her eyes shone with excitement. 'The warning says, "If the jewels of power *see* a dragon ..." The jewels couldn't *see* you because you're camouflaged, just like that boy couldn't see you!'

'But you can see me,' said Finn.

'Maybe that's because I know you so well?' Tia guessed. 'It looks like you're invisible to everyone else, even to the spell.'

'I still can't come to Drangur with you – it's too hard to camouflage myself for very long,' Finn said. 'I'm sorry. But I will practise!'

Tia left him practising looking like a fallen log and set out on the road to Drangur – alone.

Chapter Six

Into the Town of Drangur

It was a long walk to Drangur and Tia didn't reach the town until almost midday. The nearer she got, the more people she met on the road. They walked quickly and silently with their heads down. Tia did the same.

She passed through the towering town gates and onto crowded, winding streets lined with houses and shops, inns and workshops. The streets were built in a series of rising circles that led up to the castle.

Tia walked up and up, wondering why the town was so quiet. She'd never seen so many people in one place. But they didn't often talk, and when they did they looked around as though they were frightened of being watched.

Tia was so lost in thought that she almost stepped on a brindled dog sitting in the road.

'Sorry, dog,' she said and stretched out her hand to pat it. It snarled, showing its pink gums and pointed teeth. Tia jumped back. The dog slunk towards her, growling.

'Come in here, girl,' a voice said from behind her and Tia found herself dragged backwards into an inn.

A big, grim-looking woman had pulled Tia inside and now she was pushing her onto a bench at a table by an open window. She gave Tia a lump of cold meat. 'Throw that out to the dog and if you're lucky it'll forget about you.'

Tia did as she was told and the dog snatched up the meat and ran away.

'Thank you,' Tia said. 'I'll pay you for the meat.' She gave the woman a bronze coin. 'Is that enough?'

'More than enough,' the woman said. 'It'll buy you a meal as well. I'll bring it to you. And don't speak to anyone while I'm gone.'

Tia nodded, and glanced round. The customers all sat alone, staring down at their meals. Nobody smiled.

The woman returned carrying a tray of bread and cheese, a sweet pastry roll and a glass of water.

'There you are,' she said putting it on the table. She sat opposite Tia. 'Suppose you tell me what you're doing in Drangur,' she asked softly. 'I can tell you've never been before – you don't even know to beware of the beasts.'

Tia's mind raced: could she trust this woman? 'I'm a Trader...' she began.

'Careful!' the woman said. 'Don't look as though you're telling me something important; a creature might be watching to take back information to HER.' She jerked her head in the direction of the castle that loomed above them.

Tia looked round. 'I can't see any animals.'

The woman smiled grimly. 'There are cats, there are mice, there are birds that can hide anywhere. You never know what's spying.'

Goosebumps rose on Tia's arms and the back of her neck prickled as though someone – or something – was staring at her from a secret place.

The innkeeper leaned forward and asked softly, 'What are you doing here all alone, child?'

'I'm lost,' Tia whispered. 'I was separated from my people in a fog over the great plain. I've walked and walked. I'm meant to be going to Iserborg town but

I've come the wrong way.'

'You have indeed. Iserborg's a long way from here.'

'My parents will come and find me, but what can I do till then? I need to work for my keep.'

The woman shifted uneasily. 'You could always try up at the castle. No-one likes to stay there for long so there's always work to be found, especially in HER menagerie.'

'What's a menagerie?' Tia asked.

'It's where SHE keeps wild animals in cages and makes them perform. It's horrible – wolves and bears made to dance, lynx and snow leopards to do tricks. And when she's tired of them she kills them.' The innkeeper shuddered.

'That is horrible,' Tia said. 'But I need work.'

'I understand.' The innkeeper patted Tia's hand. 'When you've finished just go up to castle and say you're looking for work. And I'll prepare you a bed here for the night.'

'Thank you,' Tia said and finished off her food in silence.

The innkeeper was right; there was plenty of work at the castle, and Tia was sent to the Beast Master of the menagerie. The huge man looked Tia up and down. 'You're very small,' he said.

'I'm strong,' Tia said. 'And I can work hard.'

'The last assistant annoyed Malindra. You aren't foolish enough to do that, are you, girl?'

Tia shook her head.

'Good, because you know what happens to people who annoy Malindra, don't you?'

Tia shook her head again.

'Maybe it's just as well,' the man grunted. 'What's your name?'

'Nadya,' Tia said.

'I'm Tryg. Come with me.'

Tryg led Tia down corridors and up steps. Though Tia was used to winding tracks in the Drakelow Mountains she was confused by all the twists and turns and flights of stairs in the castle.

Eventually she found herself on a long balcony overlooking a stone-flagged courtyard with cages around the walls. The big cages held snow leopards, wolves and bears but smaller animals were kept in tiny cages piled on top of each other at the far side of the courtyard.

Tia had only seen wild animals roaming around freely and couldn't help saying, 'They look so sad!'

Tryg caught her arm, swung her round and shook

her. 'Don't ever talk about HER animals! Especially like that. You never know what might be watching or listening. Now come on.'

Tia followed him down steps leading from the balcony to the courtyard. She rubbed her arm and wondered how such a huge, strong man could be so very scared.

Tryg showed Tia how to feed and clean out the animals. They snarled and growled when she approached them. *Maybe*, she thought, *they'll trust me once they're used to me.*

She worked hard all afternoon and when she'd finished Tryg gave her two bronze coins. 'I'll give you a silver mark at the end of the week if you carry on working well,' he said.

Tia was just about to thank him when the animals began to howl and roar. The wolves and leopards circled frantically in their cages and the bears pressed themselves against the walls as far away from the bars as possible.

'SHE's coming!' Tryg said. 'Stand to one side, keep your eyes down and whatever happens, don't say a word. Understand?'

Tia nodded. It must be Malindra. At long last Tia was going to see a High Witch. A High Witch... and her aunt!

Chapter Seven

Malindra

Malindra was very beautiful. She was tall and blonde-haired and held her proud head high. She wore a white dress covered by a thick green cloak edged with black-tipped erminc. A wolf pelt wound over her shoulders as a collar and the head hung down over her right shoulder.

Perched on her other shoulder was a jackdaw. He had a thin gold chain fastened to one leg. Malindra held the other end.

'How are my animals?' Malindra asked Tryg.

The Beast Master bowed and said, 'Well, Lady.'

The High Witch lifted her hand and Tia saw a flash of green. It was the jewel of power that enabled anyone who touched it to speak to animals.

Malindra had combined this power with her magic so that she could command creatures to do as she wished. She wore the emerald in a ring which she had twisted round and the stone lay in her palm.

She pointed at a snarling snow leopard wearing a heavy collar. 'Be quiet!'

The leopard stopped growling and fell into a crouch.

'Bring him to me, Tryg,' Malindra ordered and the Beast Master unlocked the cage, attached a chain to the collar and led the crawling animal to the High Witch.

'Now bow down to me,' she said.

The leopard lowered his front legs until he was crouching with his head between his paws.

It was so undignified and sad that Tia couldn't help letting out a gasp of protest. Malindra whipped round. 'Who are you?' she demanded.

'I'm Nadya, Lady,' Tia said in a very small voice.

Malindra looked Tia up and down. 'You have Trader clothes and a Trader name but you look more like a Tulayan. How is that?'

'The Traders found me after a storm, Lady.' Tia furiously worked out her story as she went along. It might've been fun if she hadn't been so frightened. 'My parents were killed and the Traders took me in.'

'Where were you found?' Malindra asked, suddenly using the language of the Traders.

'Harvin village, near to the town of Kulafoss,' Tia replied in Trader speech. She was very glad that her friends had taught her their language and told her tales of the towns and villages of Tulay.

Malindra tugged on the chain and the jackdaw looked down at Tia.

'Shall we believe her, Loki?' she asked the bird. The jackdaw cawed. 'Very well.' The witch turned her back on Tia and went to inspect the rest of the animals.

The Beast Master gave Tia a little push and said quietly, 'Go now. The town gates will be locked soon and you don't want to get caught in here at night. I'll expect you first thing tomorrow.'

Tia slipped out of the castle and sprinted down the winding streets, thinking about Malindra as she ran. She touched the place where her locket lay under her shirt. Malindra didn't look like the picture of her mother. Just for a moment Tia was sure she could remember her mother's arms around her, making her feel safe and happy. It couldn't be – she was sister to Malindra who tormented animals for amusement and killed them for fur to decorate her clothes!

Tia ran faster. No wonder the dragons – and everyone else in Tulay – hated the High Witches. It made Tia ashamed to be related to them. By the time she reached the inn she was more determined than ever to take back the jewels, starting with her aunt Malindra's emerald.

She was very tired that night but after she'd eaten she took out her rune book and silver point pen and sketched some maps of the castle. It was so huge and the corridors were so complicated that Tia wondered if she would ever learn how to find her way around it. *But I must if I'm going to steal that emerald*, she thought as she settled down at last to go to sleep.

Tia worked hard at the menagerie, cleaning out the cages and feeding the animals. After a while they came to trust her and be soothed when she talked to them.

'You're good with the animals but don't get too fond of them,' Tryg warned. 'It'll only make it harder when SHE has them taken away.'

Tia didn't want to think about that. She thought instead about how to get the emerald back. She listened to what Tryg and the other servants said about Malindra. The witch had rooms on the third floor of the castle, one of them a laboratory where she worked her magic when the moon was full. When she made magic she took off the ring so that it wouldn't be affected by the potions and poisons she used.

I could steal the emerald when Malindra's busy with magic, Tia thought, until she learned that while Malindra worked at her magic, the great jewel was watched over by a guard who never slept. Now Tia couldn't work out how to steal the ring.

But then something happened that made her realise she had to do it soon.

Tia was sweeping out the courtyard when two men came in carrying a cage. In it were two frost-foxes. 'Oi, Tryg,' one of the men yelled. 'We got some new customers for you.'

It was the fur trappers that Tia had fought in the forest! She hid behind a stone column and watched as the men handed the cage to Tryg. The Beast Master took it and told them to collect their pay from Malindra's steward.

When the trappers had gone Tia rushed up to the frost-foxes. They were the little cubs Tia had helped escape. 'Oh, you silly things,' she said. 'Why didn't you run far away from those horrible men?'

'You'd better put them in one of the cages next to the lynx,' Tryg told her.

Tia made the foxes as comfortable as she could. 'I'll have to give you names,' Tia said. 'You're Lalli,' she told one, 'and you're Torfi,' she said to the other.

'I told you not to get fond of the animals,' Tryg said. 'SHE wants these for their fur. SHE's going to be down here any minute, inspecting them for their pelts.'

At that moment the other animals began to roar and howl and pace up and down. Malindra was coming!

This time Tia knew what to do, and she stood respectfully to one side when the witch appeared, demanding to see the cubs. Tryg bowed and took her to the cage. Malindra's eyes lit up greedily.

'Very nice. I'll add them to the fox furs I've already got and they'll make a beautiful border for my new cloak.' Her free hand stroked the grey wolf fur round her neck and the emerald glittered on her ring.

Tia had to bite her lip to stop herself from shouting out. Malindra didn't notice but Loki the jackdaw did. He peered at Tia from his perch on the witch's shoulder. Tia made herself calm and looked down at her feet. That jackdaw was dangerous – he might report her to Malindra if she wasn't very careful.

'Keep the cubs for a week, Tryg. Get the fur in tip-top condition ready for my cloak,' the witch said.

Tryg nodded and Malindra left after one last greedy look at the little white cubs.

'Tryg we can't let her do that!' Tia clutched at the Beast Master's arm.

'We've got no choice.' Tryg pushed a broom into her hand. 'Get back to the sweeping,' he said angrily.

Tia knew he was angry because he felt helpless against Malindra. Tia was angry too and brushed furiously to help get rid of her temper. She wasn't helpless – she was going to take that emerald so Malindra couldn't use it to control the animals!

Tia brushed and brushed until she felt calmer, and then she began to plan. By the time the day was over she knew what she had to do.

Back in her room at the inn, Tia got out her book and went over all the diagrams and maps she'd drawn. Tryg often sent her on errands and she'd been careful to remember everything she saw. She'd even delivered messages to Malindra's rooms.

There was only one way she could think of to get into the castle at night – she'd have to hide in the castle at the end of the day and then, when everything closed down for the night, she could creep to the third floor. Malindra made her magic under the light of the full moon. That was tomorrow night.

If Tia was going to save the fox cubs she had to go to Malindra's rooms tomorrow and find the emerald.

Chapter Eight

The Magic Laboratory

The castle was dark and full of shadows as Tia crept up the winding stone stairs to the third floor. She was using the servants' stairway and it was narrow and cold. The only light came from the moon shining through window slits in the walls.

Tia climbed steadily up till she reached a door that opened onto the third floor corridor. Flames in globes burned dimly, giving her just enough light to see her way. She stopped outside Malindra's living chambers, carefully opened the door, and slipped in.

The grand room she found herself in had a door set in each wall. To the right was Malindra's sleeping room, to the left was her dining room. And straight ahead was her magic laboratory. Sitting in front of it was a lynx. Its tufted ears were pricked up in Tia's direction and its yellow eyes glinted.

Tia reached inside her jacket and drew out a packet. She crouched down, put the packet on the carpet and opened it. The lynx crept warily to the parcel and sniffed.

'It's all right,' Tia whispered. 'It's meat I saved from my dinner in case I met an animal like you.'

The lynx began to gobble the meat down. Tia stood up slowly. The lynx took no notice and carried on eating as though it was famished.

Tia darted to the closed door, opened it a crack and shivered as a gust of freezing air billowed through.

She was looking into a large room with a domed glass ceiling letting in a flood of moonlight. In the centre of the room stood a table covered in bottles and jars filled with liquids and powders in strange, murky colours.

In the middle of the table a large crystal bowl bubbled with an icy blue liquid. In front of it, with her back to Tia, was Malindra. Both her hands were plunged in the liquid.

On Tia's right was an alcove lit by a strange green glow. *Is that from the emerald?* she wondered.

She looked all round for the guard who kept watch on the jewel but there was no sign of him. Tia thought

of Lalli and Torfi. *I have to do this for them*, she told herself firmly and, keeping her eyes on Malindra, she slipped through the door and slid round the wall to the alcove.

Inside was a plinth of black wood topped with a red velvet cushion. Resting on it was the gold ring set with the emerald that shone as green and mysterious and secret as the deepest ocean. Tia wanted to reach out and take it, but she didn't dare – the guard was in the alcove.

It was Loki. He sat on a perch, his shoulders hunched, his eyes closed. The gold chain fastened him to the plinth. Was he really asleep? Tia held her breath, reached out and slowly took the ring, her fingers touching the jewel.

'Unfasten the chain, set me free, and you can keep the emerald,' a voice said softly but quite clearly.

Tia jumped and almost dropped the ring. The jackdaw's bright black eyes stared into hers. 'You can understand me because you're touching the emerald,' he said. 'Now, are you going to free me or not?'

'I don't know how to,' she whispered.

'There's a key in Malindra's pocket. Get it and undo this.' The bird held out his leg so that Tia could see the lock.

'I can't! She'll wake up and catch me!'

'Not if you're careful,' the jackdaw said. 'She's deep in her magic trance. And if you don't do it I'll raise the alarm and she'll catch you anyway.'

Tia glared at Loki – but he'd given her no choice. She crept towards the witch. As she tiptoed closer, she felt colder and colder, and when she touched Malindra's pocket, the cloth of her dress was icy. Trying not to shake with fear and cold, Tia slid her hand down into the pocket, gripped the key and drew it out. Her numb fingers dropped it, and it rang as it hit the stone floor.

The witch's eyes flickered. Tia kept perfectly still though her heart hammered so fiercely she was sure Malindra would hear it and come out of her trance.

The witch's eyes misted over again.

Tia slowly bent down, picked up the key and crept back to Loki. He held out his leg and she slotted the key into the lock and turned it. The lock clicked open.

To Tia's surprise Loki hopped onto her shoulder. She put the ring on her finger. It was too big and she twisted it round and gripped it in her palm.

'Take the key and let's go!' the jackdaw ordered.

'Why?' Tia hissed.

'Don't argue!' Loki spread his wings in alarm. 'She'll wake up in a few minutes. We have to go!'

Tia ran and pulled open the door. The lynx barred her way, crouching and snarling.

'Let me through,' Tia said.

'I can't,' the lynx said. 'SHE's got my mate and our kittens in the menagerie. If I help you, she'll take them for their fur.'

Loki pecked Tia's ear. 'She's coming round. The magic will hold her for a little while but we've got to go now!'

Tia looked around wildly. 'There's no way out!'

'You'll have to go through the window. Now!' Loki said.

Malindra's eyes were slowly clearing. Tia pelted past her to the window and onto a balcony. She tried hard not to look down as her stomach churned and her head swam. 'Now what?' she hissed at Loki.

'There's a creeper growing under the balcony. Climb down that to the ground floor. Then you can go to the menagerie and use the gold key – it opens all the cages.'

Tia was terribly afraid of what Malindra would do if she caught her, but she was just as afraid of being up so high. She couldn't make herself move.

'Follow me.' Loki hopped onto the edge of the balcony and showed Tia the best way to go. She took a deep breath, then clambered over the balcony and gripped the creeper hard. 'I can do this,' she muttered.

'Of course you can,' Loki said.

You don't know how frightened I am of falling, Tia thought. *I feel just like I did when Andgrim dropped me all those years ago.*

She squeezed her eyes shut and began the long, long climb down. By the time she reached the ground her legs were shaking so much she could hardly stand.

'Quickly,' Loki ordered. 'There isn't much time!'

'All right!' Tia snapped and ran to the menagerie. Tryg was safely asleep in his room nearby and Tia went from cage to cage, releasing the animals.

As the last creature loped free, a shriek rang through the castle: 'My emerald! My emerald has been stolen!'

'Malindra!' Tia cried.

'We have no need to be afraid of her now,' a snow leopard growled. 'Brothers and sisters, shall we take back our freedom?'

'Yes!' the animals roared, and they ran out of the courtyard towards the outer doors of the castle. At the end of the stream of angry animals Tia saw the two frost-fox cubs running by the side of a mother lynx and her kittens.

Chapter Nine

Trapped!

Zing! An arrow bounced off the wall next to Tia. Zing! Zing! came two more. She dodged behind a pillar.

Malindra's soldiers were firing at her from the balcony. If she tried to escape with the animals, she would be out in the open – the soldiers would shoot her!

'Follow me!' Loki sailed over Tia's head.

She ran after him to the big hall crowded with servants trying to find out what was happening. Loki was wheeling above the crowd, near to a stairway. She wove through the mass of people and slipped up the stairs unnoticed.

Loki was waiting impatiently on the top step.

'Come this way and you can escape back to your DragonFriend.'

'How do you know about him?' Tia asked, astonished.

'Just before you arrived in the castle two trappers came to tell Malindra about their fight with a mighty dragon and a warrior girl. SHE didn't believe them but I could smell dragon fire on them. You have the same smell, and you are a girl who can fight.'

'I don't smell!'

'You smell of dragon,' Loki said firmly. His bright black eyes glittered. 'You are with a dragon and you've stolen the emerald. You're planning to steal back the jewels of power for the DragonQueen, aren't you?'

Tia was too amazed to do anything but nod.

'You freed me from my chain so I'm going to help you.' Loki cocked his head to one side. 'What's your real name, DragonChild?'

'Tia – and my DragonBrother's called Finn. He's waiting for me by a low cave on the edge of the forest...'

'Stop!' A soldier was behind them, aiming his crossbow.

Tia and Loki fled up a winding stone stair. Up and up, round and round Tia went until she thought she had no breath left. At the top she burst through a small door and stumbled after Loki onto the top of a turret. She slammed the door shut and leaned on it while she caught her breath. 'We're safe for now, but we're trapped,' she panted.

'I'm not,' Loki said. 'Give me the emerald.'

'No!' Tia was shocked; Loki wanted to steal the ring! After all the fine things he'd said about wanting to help her!

The door burst open. It was the soldier. 'Stay where you are!' he ordered.

Tia darted behind a flagpole in the centre of the turret. She snatched her slingshot out of her belt, slotted in a pebble, whirled it round and let the stone fly. It sent the soldier tumbling backwards through the doorway and down the stairs. Tia raced to slam the door shut again. This time she saw a bar propped against the wall and slotted it into place across the door.

'Yes!' She leapt into the air, waving her arms in excitement, and the too-large ring shot from her finger. Loki swooped down, caught it and flew away over the castle walls.

'Loki!' Tia shrieked. It was too late. He was gone. The jackdaw had stolen the ring and the soldier would report to Malindra as soon as he could.

Tia really was trapped now.

She shivered. It was still early in the night time and it was growing colder. She hauled the flag down from the pole, wrapped it round herself and huddled against the wall. What was she going to do?

'Nadya!'

The voice woke her.

'Nadya!'

Of course, Tia thought dreamily, *I told everyone my name is Nadya. I wonder who's looking for me?* She opened her eyes and saw the silver moon struggling to shine from behind dark clouds. Where was she and why was she so cold?

She remembered! She scrambled to her feet, fingers and toes numb. She had no idea how long she'd been asleep.

There was a hammering at the door. 'You may as well open it, Nadya. If you don't, my soldiers will break it down.'

'Malindra!' Tia whispered.

The door shuddered, then smashed as the soldiers

battered it down. Two of them advanced with Malindra in between them. She was white with rage and her pale blue eyes burned like ice. 'Where is my emerald?' the witch snapped.

'I don't know,' Tia said truthfully.

'Bring her to me,' Malindra ordered the soldiers

Tia ran for the flagpole and shinned up to the top. 'I haven't got your stupid ring!' she shouted.

'Fetch her down,' Malindra commanded.

The soldiers aimed their arrows at Tia.

'Don't shoot, you fools! I want her alive,' Malindra shrieked.

The soldiers tried to climb the pole and grab Tia's feet but she kicked as hard as she could and they slid back down.

'Idiots!' Malindra cried. She began to chant a spell, her eyes rolling back into her head till they showed only the whites.

Tia had never felt so alone and so frightened. The flagpole swayed and tilted over the castle walls. It was a long way down into the darkness. She closed her eyes. Malindra went on chanting.

She wouldn't try to hurt me if she knew who I am, Tia thought. *Perhaps if I tell her I'm her niece, she'll stop...*

Tia opened her eyes and saw Malindra, arms raised, the wolf's head on her shoulder looking up.

No, Tia decided. *I'd rather die than be like HER.*

Something landed with a soft thud on top of the pole. It was Loki! In his beak he had a piece of bark with runes scratched on it. Tia snatched it from him and read:

Trust Loki

Finn

Tia nodded at the jackdaw to show she understood.

Loki hopped onto the top of the turret wall and swept his wings out in a gesture that meant, *Come here*.

Below Tia, Malindra was chanting faster and Tia felt a magical tug that pulled her a little way down the pole. Loki hopped frantically, flapping his wings. Tia felt another tug.

She took a deep breath and leapt for the top of the wall.

'Catch her!' Malindra shrieked.

Tia ran round the turret wall, dodging the hands of the soldiers. One climbed on the wall and blocked her way. This time there really was no escape.

Loki dug his claws in her hair and pulled so hard that she tottered backwards. 'What are you doing?!' she yelled, trying to regain her balance.

Loki pulled her hair again. She felt her feet go from under her.

'Nooooo!' she cried as she fell backwards into the darkness.

Chapter Ten

Back to the Forest

Tia felt herself snatched up in strong scaly forelegs.

'Hold on,' a familiar voice said as she was carried swiftly away through the air.

'Finn!' Tia cried.

'Not so loud – we don't want that witch to know what's happened.'

Finn had made his skin the colour of night, all spangled with stars. Tia clung on tightly and tried to forget how Andgrim had dropped her: but though Finn was small he was strong, and carried her safely to the forest.

As soon as he landed he let go of her and she sighed with relief.

'Thank you for saving me, Finn,' she said. 'You were so brave coming all that way in spite of the spell. It must've been very hard.'

Even by firelight Tia could see Finn turn pink all over with embarrassment. 'You were away a long time and I've been practising my camouflage skills,' he said, 'But you're right, it was hard.'

Tia wanted to ask where the emerald was, and Loki, but she was stopped by a tremendous yawn. Finn nudged her towards the cave. 'Go and sleep – we'll talk again in the morning.'

Tia stumbled into the cave and was asleep in seconds.

A delicious smell woke Tia late the next morning. She came out the cave to see Finn roasting food over the fire and Loki perched on a nearby log, preening his feathers.

'Come and eat,' Finn said. 'And then you can tell us all about your adventures.'

Tia sat on the log next to Loki and tucked into the best meal she'd had for a long time. When she'd finished, Loki pecked impatiently at her hand.

'Ouch! What did you do that for?' she said.

Loki stared at her.

'Oh, you can't understand me without the emerald! Where is it, Finn?'

Finn pulled a stone away from the entrance to the cave and delicately extended one of his claws into the hole behind it. 'This seemed a safe place until you came back.'

He hooked the ring from the hole and gave it to Tia. In the forest light it shone greener than ever. Tia slipped it on and twisted the stone into her palm. At last she was able to talk to Loki again.

'Thank you, Loki,' she said to the jackdaw. 'I'm sorry I didn't trust you.'

'You'll know better next time,' he said.

'How did you find Finn?'

'You said that he was on the edge of the forest by a small cave. I was hatched here and I know the forest well. I tried a few places that seemed likely and I knew I'd found the right one when I smelt dragon.'

Tia couldn't help laughing.

'Finn wouldn't believe me at first, but I managed to convince him and guided him to the turret to get you.'

'You were both very brave,' Tia said. She smiled at Finn and reached out to stroke Loki's feathers but as she did so the ring slipped off her finger. She hurriedly put it back.

'That's such a nuisance,' she said. 'I'm afraid of wearing the ring in case I lose it but if I don't wear it I won't be able to talk to you, Loki.'

She thought for a moment. 'I know!' She took off the chain round her neck, slipped the ring onto it next to the locket, then put it back under her shirt where it couldn't be seen. She felt the emerald resting against her skin. 'Now I can talk to you,' she said.

'It's a good thing Malindra magicked the emerald smaller so she could set it in the ring,' Loki said. 'Otherwise it would be dragon-sized and too big to put on your chain.' He ruffled his feathers and shook out his wings. 'Bah. I don't like talking about HER.'

'Are you going to stay with us?' Tia asked.

'I have to go and tell my family I'm safe. But I think we'll meet again. Tell your DragonBrother goodbye for now,' said Loki.

Tia told Finn what the jackdaw had said and he rumbled a farewell.

Loki launched himself into the sky, flew away over the trees and disappeared.

'D'you think we'll see him again?' Tia asked.

'Who knows,' Finn said. 'They're unpredictable birds, jackdaws.'

'Then it's just you and me.' Tia smiled at her DragonBrother. 'I'm glad you came on this adventure with me, Finn; it's much more fun with the two of us!'

'I'm not sure I'd call it fun!' Finn said. 'But I'm glad too.' He puffed out a smoke ring. 'Can we go home now, and take the emerald to the DragonQueen?'

'No,' Tia said firmly. 'I'm going to get all the jewels back first.'

She felt for the emerald on her chain and her fingers rested for a moment on the locket. One day she would have to take the black pearl from her own mother.

'Which one are we going to steal next?' Finn asked.

'The opal; it was taken by Yordis, the High Witch of Kulafoss and that's the nearest town to Drangur. We'll set off tomorrow.'

Tia leaned against her DragonBrother and thought about the next adventure. She could hardly wait for tomorrow to come.

Tia's adventure continues in

The Opal Quest

published by A & C Black
February 2013